Words to Know Before You Read

quarter
queen
quench
quest
question
quiche
quick
quickly
quiet
quite

www.rourkeeducationalmedia.com

Edited by Precious McKenzie
Illustrated by Marie Allen
Art Direction, Cover and Page Layout by Tara Raymo

Library of Congress PCN Data

To London to Visit The Queen / J. Jean Robertson
ISBN 978-1-62169-242-3 (hard cover) (alk. paper)
ISBN 978-1-62169-200-3 (soft cover)
Library of Congress Control Number: 2012952737

Rourke Educational Media
Printed in the United States of America,
North Mankato, Minnesota

rourkeeducationalmedia.com
customerservice@rourkeeducationalmedia.com • PO Box 643328 Vero Beach, Florida 32964

To London to Visit The Queen

Counselor
Omar

Counselor
Esme

George

Nadia

Alex

Chucky

Wendy

Written By J. Jean Robertson
Illustrated By Marie Allen

Wendy is reading Mother Goose Rhymes.

CAMP ADVENTURE

"Pussy cat, pussy cat
where have you been?
"I've been to London
to visit the Queen."
"Pussy cat pussy cat

what did you do there?"
"I frightened a little
mouse under her chair."

Counselor Omar asks a question. "Shall we go to London to see the queen?"

"Yes, yes," the campers answer, jumping up and down.

"Please quiet down, campers," says Counselor Omar. "Get buckled in to take off for London. We hope to arrive at a quarter past ten."

"Wow! That was a quick trip," says George.

Counselor Omar calls, "Please line up quickly outside the bus. We want to take the Underground Tube to Piccadilly Circus."

UNDERGROUND

TRAIN STATION

11

"A circus! I like the clowns best," says Alex.

"Sorry, Alex," says Counselor Omar. "Piccadilly Circus is a big public square. We will eat lunch there. Maybe you can eat pizza, maybe quiche, maybe burgers."

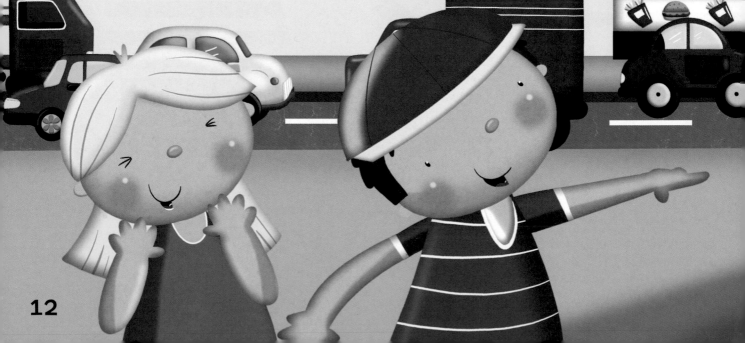

Alex asks, "Do you think we will ride on a double-decker bus?"

"Maybe," answers George. "They are really quite tall."

15

"Counselor Omar, I'm so thirsty. Can we get a drink?" asks Nadia.

"Of course. Water is the best thing to quench your thirst," says Counselor Omar.

17

"We are on a quest to see the queen!" says Wendy.

"Then come aboard for Buckingham Palace and the parade," calls the bus driver. "You can watch the queen's carriage pass."

"There she is! I see Queen Elizabeth!" says Wendy.

"The queen is quite lovely," sighs George.

"And, there is not a mouse under her chair!" laughs Alex.

21

After Reading Word Study

Picture Glossary

Directions: Look at each picture and read the definition. Write a list of all of the words you know that start with the same sound as *queen*. Remember to look in the book for more words.

queen (KWEEN): A queen is a female ruler from a royal family.

quench (KWENCH): If you quench your thirst, you drink until you are no longer thirsty.

quest (KWEST): A quest is a very long search.

question (KWEST-chuhn): A question is when you ask about something and would like an answer.

quick (KWIK): When you are quick, you are very fast.

quiet (KWYE-uht): If you are quiet, you are not making loud noises.

About the Author

J. Jean Robertson, also known as Bushka to her grandchildren and many other kids, lives in San Antonio, Florida with her husband. She is retired after many years of teaching. She enjoys her family, traveling, reading, and writing books for children. She would like to visit London someday.

Ask The Author!
www.rem4students.com

About the Illustrator

Marie Allen has had an interest in art from a young age. Art was always her favorite subject in school. She loves to create bright, fun characters for children.